WITHDRAWN

P9-BHS-113

Something for You

Charlie Mylie

Farrar Straus Giroux
New York

To Sondy

Farrar Straus Giroux Books for Young Readers
An imprint of Macmillan Publishing Group, LLC
120 Broadway, New York, NY 10271

Copyright © 2019 by Charlie Mylie
All rights reserved
Color separations by Bright Arts (H.K.) Ltd.
Printed in China by RR Donnelley Asia Printing Solutions Ltd., Dongguan City, Guangdong Province
Designed by Aram Kim
First edition, 2019
10 9 8 7 6 5 4 3 2 1

mackids.com

Library of Congress Cataloging-in-Publication Data

Names: Mylie, Charlie, author, illustrator.
Title: Something for you / Charlie Mylie.
Description: First edition. | New York : Farrar Straus Giroux, 2019. |
Summary: When a field mouse discovers that his friend is sick in bed, he is determined to make her feel better.
Identifiers: LCCN 2019011445 | ISBN 9780374312350 (hardcover)
Subjects: | CYAC: Friendship—Fiction. | Mice—Fiction. | Sick—Fiction.
Classification: LCC PZ7.1.M95 So 2019 | DDC [E]—dc23
LC record available at https://lccn.loc.gov/2019011445

Our books may be purchased in bulk for promotional, educational, or business use. Please contact your local bookseller or the Macmillan
Corporate and Premium Sales Department at (800) 221-7945 ext. 5442 or by email at MacmillanSpecialMarkets@macmillan.com.

I've got something.

oh no! you've got something, too.

get better for me

and I'll be back

with something for you.

here's a little something

for me

and a little something for you.

some for me,

some for you.

fine,
and him, too.

this part is for me

and this is mine, too.

but this will be just for you

yes,

just

for

you.

no,

no,

no!

now I've got nothing.

nothing for me,

nothing for you.

hush...

nothing except for us,

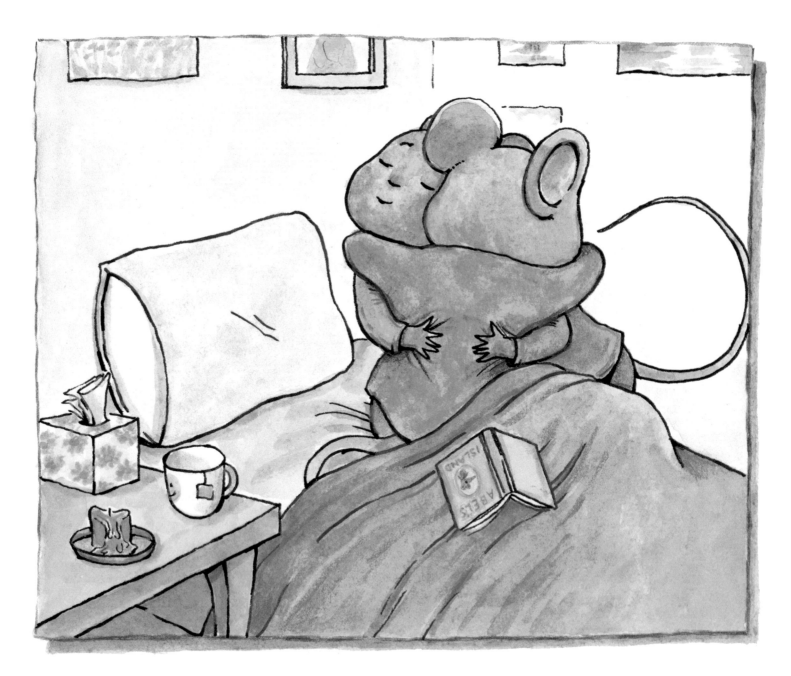

and that's enough.

CONTRA COSTA COUNTY LIBRARY

31901065581433